FEAST

ALSO BY GUILLERMO VERDECCHIA

*The Adventures of Ali and Ali and the aXes of Evil**
(with Marcus Youssef and Camyar Chai)

*Ali and Ali: The Deportation Hearings**
(with Marcus Youssef and Camyar Chai)

*Another Country/bloom**

*The Art of Building a Bunker**
(with Adam Lazarus)

*Citizen Suárez**

*Fronteras Americanas**

Insomnia
(with Daniel Brooks)

*A Line in the Sand**
(with Marcus Youssef)

*The Noam Chomsky Lectures**
(with Daniel Brooks)

The Terrible but Incomplete Journals of John D.

* Published by Talonbooks

FEAST

A PLAY

GUILLERMO VERDECCHIA

TALONBOOKS

Talonbooks
9259 Shaughnessy Street, Vancouver, British Columbia, Canada V6P 6R4
talonbooks.com

Talonbooks is located on xʷməθkʷəy̓əm, Sḵwx̱wú7mesh, and səlilwətaɬ Lands.

First printing: 2024

Typeset in Minion
Printed and bound in Canada on 100% post-consumer recycled paper

Cover image: *Still Life with Fruit and a Goldfinch* by Abraham Mignon (1660-1679). Original from The Rijksmuseum. Digitally enhanced by rawpixel.

Talonbooks acknowledges the financial support of the Canada Council for the Arts, the Government of Canada through the Canada Book Fund, and the Province of British Columbia through the British Columbia Arts Council and the Book Publishing Tax Credit.

Library and Archives Canada Cataloguing in Publication

Title: Feast : a play / Guillermo Verdecchia.
Names: Verdecchia, Guillermo, author.
Identifiers: Canadiana 20240386523 | ISBN 9781772016406 (softcover)
Subjects: LCGFT: Drama.
Classification: LCC PS8593.E67 F43 2024 | DDC C812/.54—dc23

for Tamsin, Anais, Theo, and Rosemary

If I think of somebody telling a story, I see a group of people huddled together, and around them, a vast space, quite frightening. Maybe they are huddled against a wall. Maybe they're around a fire. And somewhere, for me, in the very idea of storytelling, there is something to do with shelter. The shelter perhaps of the voyager, the traveller, who has come home, who has lived to tell the story. Or the soldier who has come back, who has survived. So there is this almost physical sense of habitation, where the story represents a kind of habitation, a kind of home. But then, inside the story, there is another kind of shelter. Because what the story narrates and tells is sheltered from oblivion, forgetfulness, and daily indifference.

—JOHN BERGER
from an interview with Susan Sontag (1983)

We can't be naive in times like this, because we are in the presence of underworld forces that will do one of two things: they will either educate us or annihilate us. And in fairy tales whenever the movement is down – and the movement culturally is down right now – you have to get underworld smart, have underworld intelligence.

–MARTIN SHAW
from an interview with Charlotte Du Cann (2017)

PRODUCTION HISTORY

Feast was commissioned and first produced at the Prairie Theatre Exchange in Winnipeg, Treaty One Territory, Manitoba, from October 10 to 22, 2023, with the following cast and crew:

MARK	Arne MacPherson
JULIA	Melanie Whyte
ISABEL/BARISTA/POSTDOC/SALES ASSOCIATE	Bailey Chin
EMEKA/DOCTOR/GEOTHERAPIST/JILANI	Ray Strachan

Director	Thomas Morgan Jones
Set Designer	David Oro
Costume Designer	Brenda McLean
Sound, Lighting, Video Designer	jaymez
Assistant Designer	Lovissa Wiens
Associate Artist	Matthew Paris-Irvine
Stage Manager	Karyn Kumhyr
Assistant Stage Manager	Ridge Romanishen
Voice Coach	Donna Fletcher
Accent Coach	Ausar Stewart
Cultural Consultant	Dr. Ben Akoh
Firearms Safety Coordinator	Dave Brown

CHARACTERS

MARK – married to Julia, father to Isabel (and Xavi), mid-fifties, probably white, white-passing, definitely (upper) middle-class, once a dreamer now a "consultant"

JULIA – married to Mark, mother to Isabel (and Xavi), mid-fifties, white or white-passing, highly practical and motivated, intelligent

ISABEL – daughter to above, twenty, and full of all those energies

EMEKA – Full name Chukwuemeka, a.k.a. Archie. Igbo Nigerian, forties? currently residing in Mombasa, probably for complicated reasons of a legal-politico-economic nature, smart, capable, constrained by circumstance

VARIOUS OTHERS – The play can be performed by four actors. Six is probably better.

SETTING

Where: The globalized world and then some.

When: Now?

PRODUCTION NOTES

Text in (brackets) is stage directions.

Text in *italics* is either direct to audience or interior.

Ellipses (...) suggest a suspension in speech or thought.

Dashes (–) indicate a line or thought is cut off.

Forward slashes (/) indicate overlapping speech.

(Shift) indicates a change in location, time, mood, lighting.

PRODUCTION STILLS

Arne MacPherson as Mark in *Feast* at Prairie Theatre Exchange, October 2023. Set design by David Oro. Lighting and video design by jaymez. Costume design by Brenda McLean. Photograph by Joey Senft.

Melanie Whyte as Julia in *Feast* at Prairie Theatre Exchange, October 2023. Set design by David Oro. Lighting and video design by jaymez. Costume design by Brenda McLean. Photograph by Joey Senft.

Bailey Chin as Isabel and Arne MacPherson as Mark in *Feast* at Prairie Theatre Exchange, October 2023. Set design by David Oro. Lighting and video design by jaymez. Costume design by Brenda McLean. Photograph by Joey Senft.

Melanie Whyte as Julia and Ray Strachan as Emeka in *Feast* at Prairie Theatre Exchange, October 2023. Set design by David Oro. Lighting and video design by jaymez. Costume design by Brenda McLean. Photograph by Joey Senft.

FEAST

(Home.)

MARK

I pack the picture last. So it's the first thing I unpack. When I get to my hotel, I'll put it on the bedside table so that it's the last thing I see when I fall asleep and the first thing I see when I wake up. That way, even if I don't know where I am, I'll know who I am.

(Shift.)

JULIA

I want to get out of the city in August.

MARK

Where do you want to go?

JULIA

Mount Kithaeron.

MARK

Where?

JULIA

It's already starting to feel thick and dirty. You can just feel how badly we've screwed everything up. It smells rank in the summer. I thought: Kithaeron. I looked it up and they had some availability.

MARK

Okay. Sounds good.

JULIA

I have this feeling, a sort of wriggling? It's what ... ? Dissatisfaction? But that's absurd. We've won the lottery, socio-economically, historically speaking. We have all we could want and more ...

Have you seen the magnolia?

MARK

No.

JULIA

It's not flowering.

MARK

It's not?

JULIA

No, it looks stunted. The flowers are barely opened. I think it was much further along last year.

MARK

Call the landscape – the ah gardening guys.

JULIA

Rosa's garden too. Everything is usually much further along by now. And did you see how blue the sky was today?

MARK

Not really.

JULIA

Too blue.

MARK

Too blue?

JULIA

Yeah. It's all out of whack.

I saw Rosa today.

MARK

Oh yeah.

JULIA

We should invite her over.

MARK

Mmmm.

JULIA

Just something simple. In the garden.

MARK

...

JULIA

You don't want to?

MARK

Sure, if you want to.

Kithaeron?

JULIA

Yeah.

MARK

Long drive. Nice, though.
Your childhood nudist playground.

JULIA

Well, it was just me running around naked.

MARK

I know. I can't imagine your father naked in the woods. Your mother maybe.

JULIA

No, she wouldn't. She used to make me "fairy necklaces" though. Flowers braided together.

MARK
The Garden of Eden. And you were Eve.

JULIA
Yeah. I played that a lot. I loved it.

MARK
We didn't let Isabel run around naked. Or Xavi.
We're not going to camp, are we?

JULIA
No, no. A cabin. I booked something called the Top of the World Suite. Presumably, one watches the world from there. It looks quite comfortable.

MARK
Sure.

JULIA
You don't sound thrilled.

MARK
No, it sounds good. I just – I don't know. I guess I'd like to go somewhere really …

JULIA
What?

MARK
Bah, I don't know. I don't know what I'm thinking. Kithaeron sounds great.

JULIA
I'm hoping the kids can come.

MARK
You think?
Is Xavi home?

JULIA
Don't think so. Work maybe?

MARK
Isabel's at the pool?

JULIA
Probably. Yeah.

MARK
What?

JULIA
Oh, you know I can't help thinking – I know you don't feel the same, but I think we made a mistake not insisting she leave home for school.

MARK
...

JULIA
I just can't help thinking that her world is small. She's making her world small, staying at home, it's a lack of ambition, lack of –

MARK
I think she puts all her ambition into the swim team. And it's a very good school here and a great swim team, very competitive and. If it was a second-rate school, then yes, it would be a concern, but.

JULIA
I know. I know. But I think for young women it's ...

MARK
Her masters. We'll kick her out for her masters.

JULIA
You all packed? Extra pair of socks in case you fall in the river?

MARK
I don't think there's a river in Beirut.

JULIA

You got your picture?

MARK

Always.

JULIA

It's very sweet that you take that everywhere. It's getting kind of old now.

MARK

I suppose. What, fifteen years? Still. It's us.

JULIA

Those days are gone.

MARK

It would be nice to have a couple days all together. Isabel will have regionals, though, doesn't she?

JULIA

Yeah. Maybe. A couple of days, though. She could take a couple of days?

MARK

Well, let's insist.

JULIA

Come with your parents or else.

MARK

Exactly.

JULIA

It's all changed, hasn't it?

MARK

Hm.

JULIA

Beirut. That could be interesting.

MARK

Could be. The Holy Land.

JULIA

I don't think Lebanon is the Holy Land, is it?

MARK

No, I don't think so. Close, though. Do you remember those atlases, those maps that were different colours for different places? We had them in school?

JULIA

Like Africa was mostly green.

MARK

Except the Sahara, yeah. We had this atlas when I was a kid, and I was fascinated by the idea of the Holy Land ... the page was pale pink ... I imagined this place where everybody was really kind and good and holy, I guess.

Hm.

JULIA

What?

MARK

Oh, just remembering that atlas. I'd like to have an atlas.

JULIA

"When I'm old I will go there."

MARK

Yeah, yeah. Close my eyes, open the atlas, "When I'm old I will go ..." plunk my finger down ... "there." Outer Mongolia or Slave Lake or Santiago de Compostela or. I loved that name. Santiago de Compostela.

JULIA

Isn't that sort of what you ended up doing? Sort of?

MARK

Sort of. But it's ... like those places don't really exist anymore.
I mean, I'm going to Beirut tomorrow. And I'm 98 percent sure
it's really not that different from – what was that place in Austria
I just went – Graz?

JULIA

Hmm.

MARK

There's no there there.

JULIA

Woah.

MARK

Yeah. I know. Heavy, man. No, it's just ... makes me feel ...

JULIA

What?
You're quite uh nostalgic this evening.

MARK

I'm not nostalgic.

JULIA

Santiago de Compostela. St. James, right? Santiago?

MARK

Yeah. He's buried there supposedly. Never did do the Camino.

JULIA

There's still time.

MARK

Is there? So many things I didn't do.

JULIA
Didn't?

MARK
Well, time is –

JULIA
Like what?

MARK
Learn to play the piano. Volunteer at a donkey sanctuary. Live in Japan? Walk the Camino.

JULIA
We can hike on Kithaeron. (sending a link over text) I just sent it to you.

MARK
Yeah, we can swim in the lake. (looking at Top of the World Suite on his phone) Looks very nice. It'll be good. A little time together.

JULIA
And maybe we should get that work on the wall done while we're away. Or the shed. I can't decide.

MARK
Do both.

(ISABEL appears.)

ISABEL
It's like some painting: the two of them sitting there. Two glasses of wine. He's got his phone, she's got her iPad. I don't know how they stand it but I guess on some level it's okay or it's good even 'cause they still seem to like each other or they talk to each other still, which is more than most of the other parents I know but still it's like I don't know a kind of slow death or something.

JULIA
Will I see you in the morning?

ISABEL
Hi.

MARK
Hi. / Wait. The wall?

JULIA
Hi, honey. How was practice?

ISABEL
Fine.

JULIA
You hungry?

ISABEL
(waving a power bar she is eating) I'm good.

MARK
A balanced diet.

Car's picking me up at five.

ISABEL
Are you going somewhere tomorrow?

MARK
Beirut.

ISABEL
(texting) Cool.

MARK
I don't know. Meetings. Conference rooms. Hotel pool, hotel room, hotel food. The local Starbucks.

ISABEL
You never see stuff ...?

MARK

No. Usually no time for that.

JULIA

Well, in ten years you'll be retired –

MARK

Ten?

JULIA

– according to my calculations – and then you'll have all the time you want. You can walk the Camino then. And when you come back, we'll sit in the backyard and drink bone-dry Mosels. We'll nurture mason bees. Read *The New Yorker* in its entirety. Grow asparagus. Explore Cinque Terre. And when it gets cold, I'll build a boat and we'll sail south.

MARK

We have a boat.

ISABEL

There's something I should be telling them like about the HEAT DEATH of the planet or something, but I don't know what it is I wanna say something that will WAKE THEM UP but also I kinda just wanna hang out which is weird but I'm gonna go with it.

MARK

We're going to go to Mount Kithaeron.

ISABEL

Oh, we went there with Nana. She loved it.

JULIA

You want to come?

ISABEL

When?

MARK

August.

ISABEL
Yeah. Maybe. I have regionals ...

JULIA
Even just a couple of days. Maybe you and your brother could drive up? It would be nice. We don't do anything as a family anymore.

ISABEL
Well, that's not my fault.

JULIA
I'm not saying it's your fault. It's just.

MARK
How things go. Hey, changing the subject, sorry. Do we have any bananas?

JULIA
I don't think so.

ISABEL
I don't know why you like bananas so much. They don't taste like anything.

MARK
They don't taste like much, it's true. But that's my breakfast: granola, yogurt, banana. Xavi eat them all? Do you know where he is?

ISABEL
No. What am I?

MARK
His sister?

ISABEL
He doesn't tell me anything. He's probably at Zozo's.

MARK
Zozo. What kind of name?

ISABEL

That's not her actual name. It's just what everybody calls her. She's super nice.

JULIA

There's a banana shortage apparently.

MARK

Yeah, 'cause Xavi eats them all. I don't ask for much. Just a banana for my breakfast. I don't know why he can't remember to leave me a banana.

ISABEL

Actually, there's a fungus that's wiping out the bananas we eat? And with climate change it's getting worse. It grows in the soil. The fungus.

JULIA

(singing)[1] Yes, we have no bananas.

ISABEL

It's demonic, anyway.

JULIA

What is?

ISABEL

Eating bananas and stuff here. At this time of year. We read this thing in class? About a guy who sells his soul to the devil?

JULIA

Faust?

ISABEL

Huh?

JULIA

...

---

1 The novelty song written by Frank Silver and Irving Cohn, performed by, among others, Benny Goodman, Spike Jones, Louis Prima, and the Muppets' Swedish Chef.

ISABEL

Yeah, this guy, Dr. Faustus, he becomes incredibly powerful, right? 'Cause he sold his soul to the devil and he does these amazing ... demonstrations. And to impress this queen he gets his personal demon to bring strawberries in the middle of winter and everybody's like amazed.

MARK

Well, I'd like a demon to bring me some bananas – I'd settle for one, just one for my brekkie.

ISABEL

No. The point is, when we get food out of season like that, it's wrong! It's necromancy.

JULIA

Black magic.

ISABEL

We don't say that anymore, Mom. But yeah, we're all basically in league with the devil now.
Anyway, good night.

(Shift.)

(A phone call.)

JULIA

Snow? In Rome?

MARK

A "Siberian Cold Front" apparently. "The Beast from the East," they're calling it. Fifteen centimetres. The Italians are losing their minds. You can imagine, the running around, the shouting, the arm waving. The falling down.

JULIA

At least you're stuck in Rome. Must be kind of beautiful. The Colosseum covered in snow.

MARK

I'm looking at a parking lot. It's not especially attractive.

It's a day before we can get a flight out, and that completely screws our schedule here in Beirut and –

(Shift to Beirut.)

(**MARK** goes through his suitcase and shoulder bag.)

What? Where's my picture?

(**MARK** removes his clothes carefully, unzips compartments, moves his laptop, pulls out a charger, rifles around inside the bags, looks at his stuff, sticks his hand back in a bag.)

Shit.

I must have left it in Rome. How?

I text the office to get in touch with the hotel. Housekeeping must have turned the picture in and could the hotel please send it back to me.

I keep looking to the bedside table where the picture should be. Now I've done it. Why didn't I just scan it and put it on my computer or phone ...? I'll do that when I get back. If I get back. That's ridiculous. The things you think sometimes.

I see my reflection in the hotel window. For a moment it looks like I'm suspended high in the air, sort of floating over the city. It's a little unnerving, dizzying.

(Another phone call.)

JULIA

What's up? You okay?

MARK

Yeah yeah, just –

JULIA

You in Beirut now? Isn't it three in the morning or something there?

MARK

Yeah, Beirut. Can't sleep.

JULIA

That's unusual.

MARK

Yeah. I don't know. Jet lag?

JULIA

You never get jet lag.

MARK

I know ... What is jet lag?

JULIA

A disruption in your circadian rhythms, your internal clock.

MARK

That's what the tasimelteon is for.

JULIA

Did you take it?

MARK

Yeah. Maybe it's finally catching up with me.

JULIA

What?

MARK

You know, flying around, crossing time zones.

It's never been an issue. I'm used to living in different calendars, time zones, teleconferencing with Zurich or Guangzhou, observing Cinco de Mayo and Lunar New Year even when I'm at home.

I've lost a lot of hours. I must have a massive deficit.

JULIA
Yeah, but you get them back on the return leg.

MARK
Do you really, though?

JULIA
It's not as if there are some hours of yours lost somewhere in the world.

MARK
You sure? I've never done the math.

I lost my picture.

JULIA
What?

MARK
The picture? Of us at the beach? I left it in Rome somehow.

JULIA
Oh no.

MARK
I had the office call them, the hotel. Asked them to send it home, to ship it back to me.

The banana was an omen.

JULIA
What?

MARK
My day started without a banana and ends without a photo. What else is going to go wrong?

JULIA
Nothing.

MARK
I know, just kidding. How was your day? How'd it go? Did you win?

JULIA
Yeah. They found in our favour.

MARK
Of course.

JULIA
Yeah, I'm seeing the arbitrator later. You know, to thank him personally.

MARK
Oh you are, are you?

JULIA
Haha.

MARK
Haha.

My reflection in the window floats away, drifts over the city like a cloud or a ghost, and eventually touches down, across town, on some amnesiac street in a gated community, and drifts into a new home, a new life, replacing someone else who has floated away.

Weird dreams too. Dusty thylacines in cages. Sad sirens and a little monkey, sitting by my bed, eating bananas, laughing at me. A nasty little sneering monkey where our picture should be.

'Cause of the snarl-up in Rome, I end up having half a day free. I have breakfast, a quick swim in the hotel pool, check email, then ask the concierge about a market. Maybe I can find a banana, see some of the Holy Land, which I know is not the Holy Land but.

(Shift.)

It's hot. The air is – you forget about air. How thick or heavy it actually is. I go from air-conditioned airplane to air-conditioned car to air-conditioned hotel room to air-conditioned conference room usually – but whoa! This real air is something.

Downtown Holy Land.

I feel a little foolish, standing here, looking around, not exactly sure which way to go.

This is a busy commercial district. I was thinking a market. The kind you see in Amex ads. With stalls and stands of fresh fruit and produce and smiling vendors hawking local goods, old, magic lamps. Maybe even people walking on water or –

The air is pressing against my body. I feel a little wobbly. I need to sit down somewhere.

(PROJECTION: A Google Maps search for "Starbucks" taken on Hamra Street in Beirut. A red pin marks the location of the Starbucks with the same description that all Starbucks locations receive on Google Maps: "Iconic Seattle-based coffeehouse chain.")

My old friend Starbucks. No matter where I go. Fukuoka. Mexico City. Seoul. The colour of the place, the smell of the coffee, the mermaid logo ... it's not the best coffee, I know. But it's familiar. Comforting.

(MARK enters the Starbucks.)

Or it is normally.

I try to let that shade of chamois on the walls soothe me ... but it doesn't.

There's lots of young people here, business people, lots of English in the air. This could be anywhere. Where am I?

Beirut. You're in Beirut.

Grande half-caff doppio misto.

What language is that? Calm down! Focus!

Me
Starbucks
Beirut
Lebanon
The Middle East
The Holy Land
Planet Earth, The Milky Way
The Univer –

(Shift to home.)

JULIA
You should go to the doctor.

MARK
It's fine. It's just jet lag, I'm sure.

JULIA
Well, why, after a decade zipping around the globe, do you suddenly have jet lag, AND ANYWAY, I've never heard of anyone walking around sideways because of jet lag.

MARK
I'm not walking around side –

JULIA
You're at an angle. You're literally off cen –

MARK
I just ... it's my balance. I feel a little –

JULIA
Go to the doctor.

MARK
I will. I will.

JULIA

When?

MARK

When I get back. If I still feel funny, I'll –
Why hasn't my picture arrived yet? From the hotel in Rome.

JULIA

What if it's serious? Where are you going now?

MARK

Richmond, Spokane, then Brno.

JULIA

Go to a clinic in Richmond.

MARK

I won't have time. It's not serious. I shouldn't have said anything.

JULIA

It's like living with a teenager again.

(Shift.)

I decide to deal with the shed. I tear it down. It feels good to swing a crowbar, to have a project. The wriggling has subsided. Maybe that's all it was. Could be hormonal too. I should go to the doctor, I suppose.

Hormonal. I don't like the word. I don't like the idea. What am I if some chemical – or whatever a hormone is – some microscopic thing can affect me like this? Does the shed really need to be rebuilt ... or is my ability to assess, decide, judge at the mercy of some hormone?

ISABEL

You okay?

JULIA

Yes. Why?

ISABEL

I thought I heard you mumbling to yourself.

JULIA

Uh-oh. / Where's Xavi?

ISABEL

Where's Dad?

JULIA

He's away.

ISABEL

Maybe he moved out.

JULIA

I think Xavi would have told us.

Just us girls then.

ISABEL

Just us. Big meet for me today.

JULIA

Right! Great!

ISABEL

... You going to wish me luck?

JULIA

Luck is for amateurs.

ISABEL

I am an amateur.

JULIA

You know what I mean.

ISABEL

It's just being nice. When someone says good luck, it just means they wish you well, you know? Like if I wish you luck when you go to court.

JULIA

I appreciate that, but wishes and luck have nothing to do with what happens in court.

I don't need luck because I'm / prepared.

ISABEL

Because you're prepared.

JULIA

I am.

ISABEL

But luck does have something to do with what happens. Like what if you get hit by a car on the way to court?

JULIA

Well ... that would probably be because someone was being careless. Me or the –

ISABEL

What about the luck that got you where you are?

JULIA

Are you hungry?

Do you win a hundred-metre freestyle 'cause you're lucky? No, you win because you put the hours in, because you work your butt off in training.

ISABEL

But I'm lucky enough to go to a school that has a good swim team, lucky I have two arms, lucky I wasn't born somewhere there's been a drought for twenty years and there are no swimming pools.

JULIA

But that's not what we're talking about. You want me to wish you luck for something you're about to do, like it's out of your hands, like you don't have agency or the –

ISABEL

... The what? The ambition?

JULIA

No. No.

ISABEL

What?

JULIA

No, nothing, I don't know what I was going to say.

ISABEL

It's just something people say. Good luck.

JULIA

People say all sorts of things, Isabel. Don't ask for luck. It's superstitious nonsense. It's right up there with ... knocking on wood and –

ISABEL

Nana knocked on wood.

JULIA

Yes, well, she wasn't always the most rational –

ISABEL

She said there were spirits in the trees and / that's –

JULIA

Exactly.

ISABEL

There might be. You don't know. You don't.

JULIA
You're changing the subject.

ISABEL
You don't know. You always act –

JULIA
Isab –

ISABEL
I have to get ready. I have to prepare. This is so not helping me prepare.

(ISABEL leaves.)

JULIA
Shit. (calling after her) You're going to do great!

(Shift.)

MARK
It's getting worse.

There's no texture to anything. Everything is smooth and slick, like sanitizing foam or aerosol gel.[2] *Cities blend into one another, a dreamy cut-and-paste remix, as if they had been designed by the same architects and planners. Has it always been like this?*

I still don't have my picture. I phone the hotel. They claim they sent it.

I feel like I might slide off the ground at any moment. My team gets a little worried. I used to come into meetings at the front of the phalanx, the spearhead. Now, I'm wedged between two colleagues who keep me upright.

---

2 See Fredric Jameson's sense of the global confusions of postmodern times in *Postmodernism, or, The Cultural Logic of Late Capitalism* or "the disorientation of saturated space" in Doreen Massey's "Politics and Space/Time."

JULIA
GO TO THE DOCTOR.

(Shift to DOCTOR's office.)

DOCTOR
Feeling dizzy? Fainting?

MARK
No, more like I might fall or slip.

DOCTOR
Bipedalism is tricky. Hugely important, of course. Fascinating. Some think we started walking on two legs because it allowed us to see over the tall grass in the savannah. What they call the "Peekaboo Hypothesis." Others, more plausibly I think, propose that walking on two feet allowed us to shade more of our bodies and therefore venture out further.

JULIA
You need a new doctor.

DOCTOR
Walking is essentially falling, only we catch ourselves by stepping. Evolution, you know. Two steps forward, one step back.

MARK
(somewhat amused) You think I'm devolving? I'm gonna start going around on all fours?

DOCTOR
No, probably just a balance issue with the ear. But it's fun to speculate. Let's get it checked.

(Shift to Starbucks.)

(BARISTA appears.)

MARK
The Flavours of Geography?

(PROJECTION: "The Flavours of Geography.")

(MARK stands at the counter with a Starbucks takeout cup that highlights their Flavours of Geography Campaign.)

BARISTA

It's our new customer experience campaign? To highlight the range of coffees we offer? Like from Central America or East Africa, and each bean has its own taste profile. Because each has a particular terroir? Terroir is like the expression of a place, the way in which specific environmental conditions? like soil, water, sunlight combine to produce the particular flavours and aromas of this bean? So, in that way, what you're tasting is the place, right? Geography. Is. A flavour. Right?

MARK

Ah.

BARISTA

I've just finished my Ph.D. in geography.

MARK

Oh, good for you.

I guess there's not a lot of work for ...?

BARISTA

I'm hoping to do a postdoc at the Centre for Avant-Garde Geography.

MARK

Oh yeah? That sounds like ...

So you can taste a place. Never thought of that.

BARISTA

You can?

(Shift to home.)

JULIA

Kithaeron's on fire.

MARK

What?

JULIA

Mount Kithaeron. It's on fire.

MARK

Mount Kithaeron.

JULIA

Yes.

MARK

Okay.

JULIA

It's ON FIRE. The forests on the mountain. They're burning. Forest fires. The entire mountainside.

MARK

Oh. Shit. Really?

JULIA

It's awful. The footage is unreal. Like a movie about the Apocalypse. But it's not. It's real. It's really happening. It's all burning up.

MARK

(looking at images on his phone) Jesus. The whole goddamn mountain ...

JULIA

Yeah. It looks like – this is not just – I can't even.

Mum used to sit with her eyes closed among the trees on Kithaeron, and when I asked her what she was doing, she'd say she was talking with the trees. I never asked her what they talked about. I should have. I'm glad she's not here to see this. It would break her heart.

The smoke from the fires makes it look like we live on another planet. One with a grey-pale orange sky and a very distant sun. It's horrifying. At first. And other times it's sort of spectacular.

ISABEL

I spend three days at Makambe's just freaking out. The world is literally on fire and people are heading out to the lake apparently and watching the fires across the water on the mountainside taking selfies ... WHAT THE FUCK, HUMANS? WHAT THE FUCKING FUCK? I hide. I don't know what to do. I miss practice. Coach freaks out. I don't care.

JULIA

The winds change direction, rain comes, the sky clears up, and we all get on with things because ... well, there are things to be getting on with. What are we getting on with exactly?

ISABEL

Everybody just goes ... back to work, back to ... like nothing happened. I can't. I'm not going back, but I can't go forward either.

JULIA

I feel hot suddenly, like my skin is heating, I sweat. Is it menopause or the planet?

(Shift.)

MARK

It's a culinary tour. You travel around, eat these great meals, really soak up the flavours of the place, really take the place in, you know? I thought since we can't go to Kithaeron and you've always wanted to go to Cinque Terre and ... I thought this might be fun.

JULIA

Yeah, okay. Let's do that.

MARK

It'll be nice to have some time together. Just us.

JULIA

It will.

MARK

This thing I've been feeling or not feeling, the lack of grip, of texture.

I've been skittering across the world. Just floating across the surface and I see everything through a window: taxi window, airplane window, browser ... I'm not connected, not in touch.

But food. Food from the place ... I could take the place into me. I could weigh myself down with a place, anchor myself, keep myself from floating away.

(Shift to Cinque Terre, Italy.)

JULIA

Questo fish is buonissimo!

MARK

Did you notice, all the staff in this place?

JULIA

The waiters?

MARK

No, the cooks. Almost all the people in the kitchen are Southeast Asian.

JULIA

So?

MARK

The visible face of the restaurant is all "Buona Sera" but the heart of the place ...

JULIA

You have something against Southeast Asians?

MARK

No! I just mean –

JULIA

They can't cook?

MARK

No.

But it's a detail that's out of place. I want a complete experience, something really ...

JULIA

What?

MARK

The thing I want to eat isn't here.

JULIA

What do you want to eat?

I know this is important to him somehow. I don't understand why exactly. It's like he wants to –

MARK

We have to go further, deeper.

(Shift.)

We eat salo and caviar with lashings of vodka.

JULIA

On the overnight train, I dream that Xavi and Isabel and their partners are all living in the shed. Like they'd been pushed out of the house, or maybe we never owned a house. Probably something I ate.

MARK

We eat suckling pig hand fed wild strawberries and organic cream by redheaded children, and then slow-roasted for three days over a fire of one-hundred-year-old rosewood shavings.

(Shift.)

JULIA
I'm going to cut my part of the trip a little short.

MARK
What?

JULIA
I'm ready to go back but you can stay and –

MARK
Is something wrong?

JULIA
No, no, it's not that. It's easy to change the ticket and I want to get back and do some things at home, and ...

MARK
Really? Are you sure?

JULIA
Absolutely.

MARK
I thought you wanted to be out of town in August?

JULIA
I did. But now I want to go home.

MARK
This feels ... are you sure there's nothing wrong? You haven't enjoyed ...

JULIA
I have. I have. It's been great. Really. I'm glad we came.

MARK
But.

JULIA

No but. I just want to go home. And you want to stay. And we are adults and we don't need to do everything together.

MARK

If you're sure there's nothing –

JULIA

Absolutely.

(JULIA leaves with her suitcase.)

MARK

As soon as Julia goes, I run to the sketchier corners of the gastronomical world. Looking for the real goods, the dirt under the toenails of the water buffalo whose milk made the mozzarella.

(A phone call to JULIA.)

Hi, honey, look, I'm actually going to fold a couple of work trips into this if that's okay. It's just easier if I stay here rather than fly back home and with the time difference and everything and ...

I lose track of time. Days run together, light then dark, rain then sunlight, a blur...

(Shift back home to JULIA and ISABEL.)

ISABEL

Do you remember *National Geographic*?

JULIA

The magazine?

ISABEL

Yeah.

JULIA

Sure ... we had a subscription. When you and Xavi were little.

ISABEL

Yeah.

JULIA

You used to cut them up for school projects. They had wonderful photography.

ISABEL

...

JULIA

Do you remember those social studies projects? You were so careful about laying the pictures out on the bristol board. Remember bristol board?

ISABEL

...

JULIA

Are you hungry?

ISABEL

Why do you always ask if I'm hungry?

JULIA

Well, you don't always eat regularly and you know it makes you – there's lots of leftovers.

ISABEL

Dead animal?

JULIA

No, there's chickpea curry and some of that really yummy dal –

ISABEL

I'm not going to have kids.

JULIA

... Oh.
What do you ...?

ISABEL

I'm not going to have kids.

JULIA

You're not going to have kids?

ISABEL

I won't.

JULIA

... You mean because you're gay? There's lots of ... you could adopt, or, you know, get a donor or –

ISABEL

God.

JULIA

Anyway, you're too young to be thinking about kids, about having kids, you have a whole lot of life ahead of you before you –

ISABEL

No, I don't. I don't. I don't have a whole lot of life ahead of me! That's what I mean!

JULIA

Honey ... what's ... what's wrong? Sweetheart, why are you so upset?

ISABEL

Why the hell would anyone bring kids into the world – what for? So they can drown when the sea level rises or starve 'cause of food scarcity or –

JULIA

Woah. Woah. Honey, calm down.

ISABEL

Why the hell how the fuck can I calm down? Do you not get it? No FUTURE. No future. My life has been stolen –

JULIA

Isabel, honey. You're really upset.

ISABEL

Of course, I'm upset! Why aren't you upset?

JULIA

I understand, of course it's upsetting. Of course.

ISABEL

You understand, that's really helpful.

JULIA

But –

ISABEL

There is no BUT, Mom. The world is going up in flames but what? Look on the bright side?

JULIA

I just mean that being – that getting so worked up makes everything seem worse. It's harder to deal with a problem if we let our feelings get –

ISABEL

Deal with? Like your generation dealt with the problem?

JULIA

My gener – Isabel.

ISABEL

We've known about global warming for more than forty years! Almost your whole life!

JULIA

We didn't know –

ISABEL

Exxon knew about it in 1977. They had scientists who wrote about the effects of fossil fuels way back in 1977.

JULIA

Well, they didn't tell us about it. Isabel, we – our house uses green electricity, we have Bullfrog. We've been / recycling for –

ISABEL

Like that makes a difference.

JULIA

We have an electric car! Your father was one of the first people in the neighbourhood to stop using weed killers. I was arrested at Temagami. My generation? My generation started Greenpeace. Started Sea Shepherd. Earth First. My generation did all kinds of things.

ISABEL

Not enough. Not enough. Droughts are getting worse. Glaciers in the Himalayas that provide water to like two hundred million people are disappearing. Storms are getting worse. More heat waves. FOREST FIRES? Hello! Coral reefs wiped out. Bees wiped out! The planet, Mom!

And Dad! Flying around the whole world. Every week, he's flying off somewhere, destroying entire rainforests all by himself.

JULIA

He – it's his work. He has to.

ISABEL

Well, his work is killing us.

(Silence.)

JULIA

Oh, darling. I'm sorry. I didn't mean to argue. I – I felt attacked. Yes. It's terrible. It's a nightmare. I know.

(Silence.)

ISABEL

It's not your fault.

I'm not stupid. There's nothing one person can do. It's not about individuals making changes. It's not about Bullfrog Power or ... reusing plastic bags anymore.

I ah I was looking at an old *National Geographic*, and the pages are smooth and shiny and thick, and the pictures are sooo beautiful and ... it was like a paradise. I used to think when I was little, I used to think one day I would go to those beautiful places, and I would see sea horses, an actual real sea horse, in the wild, not an aquarium, and axolotls, those weird little salamanders in Mexico City and they're almost wiped out. There's only one lake in Mexico City where they live and there used to be a thousand of them per square kilometre and ten years later, they found two. Two. Two in the whole lake! And I used to dream that I'd study them and learn ... to even talk to them ... and I'd be somewhere where it was so thick and green the air would be green, and it was like I thought the planet was like the Garden of Eden or something and it's all gone. I'll never, we'll never have that again.

Mommy, I'm so sad. I don't think I can stand it.

(Shift. Another phone call.)

MARK
Yeah, quarantined.

JULIA
Really?

MARK
We're fine but have to isolate for five days.

JULIA
Who still does that?

MARK
They're very serious about it. It's just this province, I think. Not the whole country, though there's rumours they might close the border.

JULIA

Come home as soon as you can.

MARK

Definitely.

I think I am floating away. All that time I spent at hotel windows, staring down at whatever city, worrying about floating away. It's what I actually wanted.

(Shift to Mombasa.)

(EMEKA appears.)

EMEKA

There is a white man, laughing, staggering and spinning around in the middle of the street, like a drunkard. But he's not. Someone is far from home. He'd best be careful.

Come in out of that rain, friend. Something to warm you up? Are you all right? What is so funny?

MARK

Ah, thank you. That's some rain! I was just remembering getting lost once in Beirut. Ever been there? No? Well, me neither really, but I was sort of lost briefly there, panicked a little because it all seemed very familiar and yet I didn't have any idea where I was and now just now I thought well, look at me now! I guess we're not in Kansas anymore!

EMEKA

No Dorothy, you're definitely not in Kansas. Perhaps I can be of some assistance?

(EMEKA hands him a business card.)

MARK

(reading the card) Import Solutions.

EMEKA

O, not that one. Here.

MARK

(reading the card) Expert?

EMEKA

O! No! How did that –? Here.

MARK

(reading the card) Logistics.

EMEKA

Yes. I manage the flow of things from one point to another.

MARK

And this place?

EMEKA

Yes, O. I am the proprietor. It settled a ... debt of sorts and forms part of my diversified portfolio. I have a hand in hospitality, in sports management, and –

MARK

Sports management?

EMEKA

A football club.

MARK

Soccer?

EMEKA

We didn't play many matches. Mostly we provided security for politicians and Big Men.

I also run a variety of consultancies. I have advised Russian investors on their investments. And American operatives with their operations.

MARK

Operatives?

EMEKA

Almost certainly CIA.

MARK

Really? What did you do for the CIA?

EMEKA

Ah, if I told you that I'd have to kill you.

Only joking, my friend. Only joking.

MARK

Ha! Okay, what ah what did you do, then?

EMEKA

...

MARK

Okay.

EMEKA

You're looking askance.

MARK

I'm what?

EMEKA

Looking at me dubiously.

MARK

Am I?

EMEKA

I'm a fixer, my friend. What can I fix for you ...? You are making a movie here? You need tents, tigers, Maasai extras, leave it to me.

MARK

No, no, I'm not making a movie.

EMEKA
What brings you to this corner of the world, Mzungu?

MARK
Oh ah I'm – I was just eating local, I got a tip, a recommendation, about a local, some kind of fish ... It was a bit like a hairbrush baked in sand and fat but ...

EMEKA
All the fish is frozen today. From China. Everything is from China now. You see those towers going up, the cranes, construction, new highways, it's all Chinese my friend! Welcome, our new Asian overlords! And may they hire me soon!

MARK
They were supposed to take me back to my hotel, but they just drove me around in a big circle and dropped me off here ...

EMEKA
Mshomoroni is not always welcoming at this hour. You're lucky I found you, O!

MARK
I guess I am.

EMEKA
So, Mzungu, you're hungry.

MARK
How did you know?

EMEKA
Ah.

What can I fix for you?

MARK
... I'd love a banana.

EMEKA

A banana?! Haba! Just a banana? My friend, the Cavendish, the white man's banana, is endangered. A rarity. I can get you one but for that money let me arrange something a little more substantial ...

MARK

And so, Archie –

EMEKA

It's the bar that's called Archie's. After the former proprietor. My name is Chukwuemeka, like Carney Chukwuemeka.

MARK

Who?

EMEKA

Midfielder. Plays in the Premier League.

MARK

Don't know him.

EMEKA

You don't follow the footie?

MARK

What does, what's Mzunga?

EMEKA

A term of affection for white man.

MARK

Archie becomes my fixer. He arranges everything: accommodations, travel, fresh clothes, and the most extraordinary culinary opportunities.

(Shift.)

EMEKA

Baby sea turtles with a wormwood salad in an alley in Michoacán.

MARK

That sounds risky?

EMEKA

All part of the experience, the flavour. But don't worry. I will arrange a guide.

(Shift.)

MARK

Adders in laudanum at the Peninsula Hotel in Hong Kong.

EMEKA

A helicopter will deliver you to the rooftop ...

(Shift.)

MARK

I don't feel so wobbly here. It feels like somewhere. And Archie keeps arranging these amazing meals.

EMEKA

Mzungu. Some days I feel sorry for him. He flies to Japan to eat mushrooms and claims he can taste the sadness of autumn and that he can remember a childhood in a Japanese village collecting crickets. Is he mad? It's not exactly honourable to make money from this man's ... unhappiness? His foolishness?

What is wrong with the white man?

O Abeg! Na idiot talk be dat. No dey worry about Mzungu! Him lay in the bed wey him make. And we are making money after a very long dry spell.

(Shift to home.)

JULIA

Geese honking, circling the property. Why? What do they see? What do they know? Is it the low clouds, the constant rumble of thunder? What are they telling me?

(Shift to Archie's.)

EMEKA
(bringing MARK a beer) Two. Girls.

Mzungu has a luxury hotel in Nyali, but he comes around every day. He has been here for weeks now.

MARK
Yeah?

EMEKA
In England. Private school. My eldest, Ijedinma, she will be a lawyer. And Ndidi, she is in third form. She says, Daddy, I want to build bridges. I say, yes, girl, yes. Change the world!

MARK
England?

EMEKA
Oya, the part of me that is still colonized thinks that's where one goes for a real education. I want to believe in this continent, but I am no fool. I want my girls to have options. If they want to come back here, to build bridges, I say, yes, wonderful, but if they say, Daddy, I am marrying a Harley Street specialist, I also say wonderful! Live your life. And bring me to live with you! In your big house in the Home Counties!

MARK
You'd live in England?

EMEKA
England. Finland. Anywhere you can get ahead on your own effort. Anywhere the corruption index is above sixty.

MARK
You ever think of emigrating? Somewhere –

EMEKA
Almost daily. It's not so easy for some of us.

MARK

Right. Of course. It must be very … frustrating.

EMEKA

Patience will cook a stone. An opportunity is waiting for me somewhere, someday.

MARK

Private schools? Must be expensive.

EMEKA

Their uncle is a Big Man. With business in England. He helps a little. And they have some scholarships. They work very hard. And everything I earn, everything, goes to my girls, their schools. My own needs are few.

MARK

And their mother?

EMEKA

A great Yoruba beauty and a big mistake. And you?

MARK

Yeah. Two kids. Xavi and Isabel. Isabel is the oldest, two years older than her brother. They're both in school.

EMEKA

Don't you miss them?

MARK

Well, they have their own lives now. You know, as they get older, they need you less and less. And Julia, she has a very demanding position and she's got so many projects … I thought actually we should come here together some day. I think she'd love it.

EMEKA

He should be with his wife and children. He needs them even if they don't need him.

A single bracelet does not jingle, Mzungu.

MARK

This is just a little detour, an extended vacation. So ... what else have you got for me?

EMEKA

Still "hungry"?

MARK

Something ... special.

EMEKA

So I suggest the ne plus ultra of extreme cuisine.
Neurotoxin gastronomy.

MARK

Like fugu?

EMEKA

Eh eh. No now! Pufferfish is for tourists. If you dey serious, if you dey serious serious, if you want wetin you say you want, you want a golden dart frog.

MARK

A dart frog?

EMEKA

The most poisonous creature in the world. But you must only eat the legs! And it must be correctly prepared! Very few people have ever eaten this. Even fewer can make it. Very delicate. High-level negotiations required. Special visas.

MARK

Yeah. That sounds like something.

(Shift.)

JULIA

Two days of biblical rain. The ground won't absorb any more water, and it's pooling on the patio. Storm drains are overrun, cars abandoned in underpasses, and now

I can see water coming in through the basement windows
pouring down the wall

water comes in over the top of my boots
cold dirty water swirling and rising

dark water full of detritus of unnamed floating things

so loud
I feel the pipes pounding
hear water swirling and sucking
the ground groaning and choking
the foundations and joists creaking
other things too
living things crying out
worms and bugs drowning and mice scurrying for higher ground
coyotes running from their dens with pups in their mouths
and homeless people dragging their sleeping bags
pushing their carts
carrying their dogs
trying to get somewhere anywhere dry
fish disoriented and confused drowning how can that be can fish drown
but they are
and whales desperately calling to one another across the oceans
but not a single axolotl not one
trees uprooted and crashing
icebergs collapsing
shorelines swallowed

where are the kids

I try to call on the water spirits I can remember
on the undines and the selkies on Mami Wata and the rusalki and all the Haitian mermaids and the naiads and the nereids on Achilles's mother Thetis and
Yemayá the mother whose children are fish
and I call on my mother and the myriad sprites she believed in
and ask them
to save me my children our home

but they can't hear me or won't listen or I don't know how to speak to them

standing there with the water pouring into my rain boots a little book floats past
Sun Tzu's Art of War:
In chaos, there is opportunity, it says.

(Shift.)

EMEKA
My friend! What happened?

MARK
I got robbed. Somebody just –

EMEKA
Are you / all –

MARK
He had a knife.

EMEKA
Are you hurt? / What's wrong with your hand?

MARK
No. I fell.

EMEKA
You're sure you're not hurt?

MARK
No, just, I fell and hurt my leg, my hand is bleeding but –

EMEKA
Where?

MARK
(indicating his hand) Here.

EMEKA
No. Where did this happen?

MARK
Just down the street, a –

EMEKA
Did you see –

MARK
Just a guy with a knife. Skinny guy. He got my wallet. I gave him my wallet.

EMEKA
That was wise.

MARK
All my credit cards, my ID, everything.

EMEKA
You can get all that back.

MARK
What was I thinking? That I'm invisible or – he had a goddamn knife. I could be dead.

EMEKA
Let me get you a drink.

MARK
I have to phone the bank. He took my phone.

EMEKA
Do you have your passport?

MARK
I don't carry that with me.

EMEKA
That's good.

MARK

I have to cancel my credit cards.

EMEKA

All right. Use my phone. This one. No. Wait. This one. Ah. No, here, this one is better. Different plans, different rates, you understand. And sometimes one network is out, I have options.

MARK

God. GOD. I can't – my hands are shaking.

What the hell am I doing? Archie. This is crazy. He's a skinny little guy, in a kind of a nylon jacket. I mean it's so dark, all the lights are out around here. I just saw the knife first, and it was like I didn't even recognize it like it had nothing to do with me. I could be dead.

EMEKA

You're okay.

MARK

I'm a million miles from home. Chasing around trying to what? I think I've gone a little crazy, Archie.

(EMEKA brings him a drink.)

I'm completely off the map. Just floating away, right off the surface of the planet.

EMEKA

You are far from home, yes.

MARK

I don't even know when the last time I spoke to my kids was. I don't know when I last saw my son. I think maybe he moved out and I didn't notice. What do I think I'm doing here? I'm sniffing around for the next intense thing to eat, like a bloodhound tracking a convict through the tangled forest. Except I am the bloodhound and the convict –

EMEKA

O! Breathe. Drink.

Mzungu, no catastrophe will tear up your life. You will never ask for someone else's cast-off clothes or wear boots too big for your feet. You will not sleep in abandoned buildings or in railway yards. You will never worry about having enough money or water or rice, whether soldiers will track you in the forest or police will break down your door to shoot you in the back or just beat you, rob you, and throw you in the ditch.

What is wrong with the white man that he must invent sorrows, troubles, afflictions? That he must come traipsing around the world, remaking everything in his image, claiming everything, buying up every last damn thing, and still dem no dey satisfied, still dem dey wan chop and chop. I no understand, O!

And I don dey vex
I feel that anger that comes on me when I think on the fundamental injustice of every goddamn thing
that anger bigger and darker than Sambisa Forest
that anger big as Africa
that anger I must swallow down if I'm not to go mad mad mad, if I'm to be of any use to my girls, if I'm ever to find my way out ... not Mzungu's fault ... we each have our hungers.

It was just a garden-variety robbery. Unfortunate, but not as bad as it might have been. Consider it a kind of tax the locals collect. The malfeasant, what was –

MARK

God. Okay. Okay. That was just a rush of adrenaline or something. I suppose there's no point in calling the police?

EMEKA

Mmmm. I'd prefer if you don't. My situation here is ... irregular.

MARK

...

Okay.

EMEKA

Let us make the necessary phone calls and straighten out your credit cards. You will stay here tonight.

MARK

Here?

EMEKA

I have a room in the back.

MARK

A room?

EMEKA

I live back there.

MARK

Oh. No no no. I can't –

EMEKA

Yes yes yes, you can.

MARK

I should go. I should be –

EMEKA

To your hotel? Now? / How?

MARK

Yeah, but I mean home. I should go home. I mean, really, what do I think I'm doing here?

EMEKA

But you know.

MARK

I don't, I really don't ...

EMEKA

You're seeking ... something to stop that gap, to soothe that ache. A kind of reward. You want ... more.

MARK

...

EMEKA

That's what it is to be alive, isn't it? To want more.

MARK

Do you?

EMEKA

Mzungu, do you think I am satisfied in this broken-down bar in this broken-down neighbourhood in this broken-down country? Of course I want more, much more, and I'm going to get it. If not for me, for my girls.

Listen, cancel your cards. Then rest here. In the morning, I will retrieve your wallet.

MARK

What?

EMEKA

Skinny fellow with a knife? PSG logo on the jacket?

MARK

I don't know. A dark nylon jacket.

EMEKA

Mhm. Voice like pepper and honey?

MARK

Yes! You know him.

EMEKA

I know his sister. You take the bed. I'll sleep out here tonight.

MARK

I don't want to take your bed.

EMEKA

Haba! Don't be so polite. You need a good night's rest. In the morning everything will be better. Let me find you something to sleep in.

Oh, I almost forgot. I have your reservation. For the frog.

MARK

You do?

EMEKA

They confirmed today. A rising star on the poison-cookery circuit. The exact details including the location will be revealed upon payment to their numbered account.

MARK

... You're very good at this.

Thank you, Archie.

I really appreciate this. Everything. I hope some day I can do something for you.

EMEKA

Between friends even water drunk together is sweet enough.

But wait till you see what I charge for the bed ... and the linen. Pillow? Extra, my friend. Toothbrush? Very expensive, O.

(Shift.)

(PROJECTION: "The general who wins the battle makes many preparations before the battle is fought. The general who loses the battle has made few."
—Sun Tzu, *The Art of War*)

JULIA

The flood is a four-alarm alarm that shakes me out of the deep sleep I've been in. Fire on the mountain. Flood on the plain. What other sign am I waiting for? A plague of poison frogs?

I need to prepare. For the worst. Get rid of what doesn't serve anymore and look forward.

But I'm not going to move to New Zealand like those Silicon Valley fundamentalists. What I need to do is fortify this *place, make it secure. This is My Forever Home.*

So: FUCK YOU, GAIA.

This is not yet the end of the world. This is an opportunity. I will Renovate. Make it better. Make it safe. Safe as houses.

(Shift to an elevator, Colombia.)

MARK

(singing, perhaps a little like "Largo al Factotum" - Figaro! - but melancholy, dreamy) Julia, Julia, Julia.

EMEKA

The frog did not agree with Mzungu, O. My Colombian associate has found him collapsed in the hotel elevator, delirious. Singing tunelessly to himself.

MARK

(scrambling any number of melodies together) Are those pearls in your eyes, Julia Julia?

I can't seem to recognize shooby doo dooby da.

Windy voice, call me ...

EMEKA

I have him airlifted to the nearest hospital and call his wife to let her know there's been an accident. I double-check the contract to make sure he signed the indemnity and hold harmless clauses. He did.

(Shift to hospital.)

MARK

(coming to) *Julia. She heard me singing! But that's impossible, isn't it? Yet, there she is. Sitting beside my ... bed? In a hospital ward? In ... the foreign country ... where I went ... to eat ... a poison frog.*

JULIA

It's been a good run.

MARK

...

JULIA

Everything's changed and we should recog –

MARK

What? What's changed?

JULIA

You've changed.

MARK

I've changed?

JULIA

Well ... what do you call this?

MARK

I ... got ... food poisoning and I've / been –

JULIA

Food – you've been unconscious for days. What did you eat?

MARK

Some bad ... fish / or –

JULIA

No, food poisoning is not the issue. I mean, where have you been – you, what? You had a fugue state or –?

MARK

I was quarantined. I called you –

JULIA

That was ages ago.

MARK

I've been working.

JULIA

Your office had no idea where you were. You were working here? Staff found you in the elevator of a broken-down hotel in a broken-down little town on – I mean thank goodness your dealer called me / to tell me you'd been hospitalized –

MARK

Dealer?

JULIA

Your Nigerian agent. Whatever he is. Nice guy. Chukwuemeka Okonkwe.

MARK

Archie? He's Kenyan.

JULIA

The bar is called Archie's. His name is Chukwuemeka like the midfielder, and he's Igbo, from Nigeria, living in Kenya illegally at present.

MARK

How do you know all this?

JULIA

I ask questions.

I didn't even mind. I liked it. That you were away. I liked having the bed to myself, the house to myself, mornings, evenings to myself. We had a flood. I waterproofed the basement. I can't tell you how ... how ... energized I felt.

MARK

A flood?

JULIA

In the basement. I redid it. All. Waterproofed. *Flood*proofed.

MARK

Oh. God. Thanks. I ah would have helped, I didn't –

JULIA

I feel safe ... It's good.

MARK

Good? This is good?

JULIA

Let's look at this objectively. When were you planning on coming back?

MARK

Okay, yes, I admit ... I've been ... remiss. I haven't been communicating well ...

JULIA

I'm not blaming you. I'm not being reactive. I'm being proactive. I'm making a change.

MARK

You left. When we were on our holiday. You left.

JULIA

But ... I wasn't I didn't mean it as anything.

MARK

You're the one who –

JULIA

Let's not start with you this, I that. That is honestly not the point. There's no blame. It's just something that is happening. It's a reality that is larger than us.

MARK

"Something happening"? You – I don't understand this.

JULIA

Everything is changing. Don't tell me you can't feel it. The kids. The whole world. Something has ended.

MARK

This is like – you might as well be speaking Basque.

JULIA

This doesn't have to be a drama. We could just be sensible about this.

MARK

Sensible? I almost died, you know. Have you met somebody?

JULIA

No, I haven't met. This isn't about anybody else. It's about me.

MARK

What about me? This isn't about me?

JULIA

I mean there's no one else. I haven't "met" anybody.

MARK

... Do you love me?

JULIA

... Yes.

MARK

So ... why?

JULIA

We're not growing. We're not building. We have no project together.

MARK

...

JULIA
: And if we're not growing, then what are we?

MARK
: A family.

JULIA
: We're not a photograph.

MARK
: ... Look, I'm going to get better. Get help.

JULIA
: It's time. That's all. All things must pass.

MARK
: ... That's ... that's a George Harrison album!

(Shift.)

JULIA
: *Looking at the city from the airplane is soothing. The world from above. It makes sense from up here. The patterns, the arrangements, the flows. You can see how it all fits together. Something is coming clear.*

(Shift to home.)

ISABEL
: So ... I'm quitting the team.

JULIA
: You want to quit?

ISABEL
: I did. I quit.

JULIA
: Why? Did something happen?

ISABEL
I don't want to do it anymore.

JULIA
You don't – but you've felt like this before and it's always –

ISABEL
Yeah. But this time I'm going to listen to how I feel.

JULIA
But you love competing, you love swimming.

ISABEL
I haven't loved it for a long time.

JULIA
...

ISABEL
I loved water. Being in the water.

How many hours have I? Twenty hours a week, sometimes more. For years. Thousands of hours. Preparing. For what? To win races? What's the point of that? I'm tired.

JULIA
Well, of course, but –

ISABEL
No. I'm deep tired. In my bones. My heart. I feel like I'm a thousand years old.

JULIA
Honey.

ISABEL
...

JULIA
What's wrong?

ISABEL

It's not just swimming. I've decided to leave school. And I'm – I can't keep going to school like it's a necessary, like there aren't more important things for me, for all of us, to be doing.

JULIA

What is more important than school?

ISABEL

Saving the world.

JULIA

...

ISABEL

I'm joining – I've joined, I'm volunteering with a climate-justice NGO.

JULIA

...

ISABEL

I know you think this is a mistake, or that I'm not thinking clearly or ... but I've thought about this for a long time. It's what I have to do. It's not even a choice, though it is a decision. It's like I'm being called, and I'm answering that call.

JULIA

... Isabel. You sound ...

ISABEL

What?

JULIA

Finish the year, there's not that much left and if you still feel –

ISABEL

If I still feel like it's important to save the world? To do something?

JULIA

...

ISABEL

Mom. I'm just telling you. I'm not asking for advice or – I'm telling you what I'm doing.

JULIA

What are you going to do? With this NGO?

ISABEL

They work with people who have been displaced by the climate crisis. Not everyone can just floodproof their house or whatever. Most people are forced out ... one hundred million of them, more, around the world. Their land is flooded or turns into desert, homes are destroyed, livestock –

JULIA

I know what happens, Isabel.

ISABEL

You do? Do you? You know?

JULIA

... I'm just asking what you are going to do.

ISABEL

Shorelines are flooding. People are drowning. And I can swim.

JULIA

...

ISABEL

I'm leaving tomorrow.

JULIA

Tomorrow? Where?

ISABEL

Ottawa.[3] And then Vanuatu.

JULIA

Vanuatu. Isn't that a million miles away?

ISABEL

I mean, eventually. That's where I hope to go. They use sailboats. To travel there, I mean.

JULIA

Tomorrow. How long have you known? That you were going to do this?

ISABEL

A while.

JULIA

But you're just telling me now.

ISABEL

Yeah, I'm just telling you now. Things are different now, Mom. All the old ways of doing things are gone.

JULIA

Like asking your parents –

ISABEL

I'm not asking.

JULIA

Considering your parents, what they think, what they need, what they feel –

ISABEL

Honestly, Mom? What we feel isn't important anymore. And what do you need? What do you really need that I can give you?

---

3 Or somewhere else, depending on where the play is produced.

JULIA

...

ISABEL

...

JULIA

I need to know you're safe. I need to know that you're okay, about you, your life, your –

ISABEL

This is my life. I'm telling you all about it. And nobody's safe anymore.

JULIA

What does Makambe say?

ISABEL

She's coming too.

JULIA

She's leaving school too.

ISABEL

We have to do something.

JULIA

And you don't think maybe you should ... wait? If you get your degree then –

ISABEL

When the world goes up in flames, having a B.Sc. won't make any difference.

JULIA

...

One hundred million people? Where are they going?

ISABEL

Wherever they can.

JULIA

One hundred million.

ISABEL

More. It'll happen here too. It's fucked, Mom, totally.

JULIA

Isabel …

ISABEL

What?

JULIA

I love you.

ISABEL

You won't talk me out of it.

JULIA

And I'm very proud of you.

ISABEL

…

JULIA

…

ISABEL

Will you tell Dad for me?

JULIA

No, honey, that's something you have to do.

ISABEL

When's he coming home?

JULIA

I'm not sure.

ISABEL

Where is he?

JULIA

He's ... we ... I'm not sure.

ISABEL

What's going on?

JULIA

Oh ...

ISABEL

He hasn't been home for ages. Did you guys split up?

JULIA

... He's very busy and he got sick actually but he's okay and ... well, yes, we are ...

ISABEL

What? Everything is just ... falling to pieces.

... Will you hug me?

(JULIA and ISABEL hug.)

JULIA

Don't go.

ISABEL

Mom.

JULIA

Don't go. Stay here. We'll be safe here.

ISABEL

Mom.

JULIA

I don't want you to go.

ISABEL

It's okay. You'll see.

JULIA

(holding her in a hug) Stay. Stay. Stay.

(Shift.)

MARK

I'm clinging to my Starbucks takeout cup. So jittery. Look at the logo. Concentrate on the mermaid. I told Isabel we'd go see The Little Mermaid *– the sculpture – in Copenhagen for her tenth birthday. Another thing I didn't do.*

(**PROJECTION:** Starbucks' logo as it appears on their cups.[4])

Not a mermaid actually. She's a siren. The feathery things along the side are her two tails. It's hard to tell in this version.

(**PROJECTION:** Starbucks' original logo, designed by Terry Heckler in 1971. The logo is brown rather than the company's current green. The company's name makes a circle around the edge and at the centre of the circle is a bare-breasted, two-tailed siren.)

It used to be quite clear. She had two tails, breasts, a belly button. She's shaggy.

Then:

(**PROJECTION:** Starbucks' logo as adapted in 1987 after the company was bought by Il Giornale, a competing company. The brown of the original

4 For a more corporate version of this logo timeline, Starbucks provides their own: archive.starbucks.com/record/the-evolution-of-our-logo

logo changed to green and the siren becomes more stylized.)

They cleaned her up. Her hair covers her breasts. Her tails become less ... tail-like.

Till we get:

(PROJECTION: Starbucks' logo as updated in 1992. Similar to the 1987 logo, but zoomed-in on the image of the siren.)

Why do I know more about that logo than I do about Julia's longings? I know it better than I know the colour of her eyes.

(PROJECTION: "I have heard the mermaids singing, each to each, I do not think that they will sing to me."[5])

Are there any sirens left? Haven't we scraped the ocean floor clean?

(Airport announcement perhaps in some extinct language – Latin or Coptic;[6] MARK picks up his bag and moves away.)

(Shift.)

JULIA

I get home from work and walk the perimeter. I tell the trees about Isabel's decision and how I'm suddenly alone. The trees have nothing to say to me.

I go down to the basement and listen to the drywall, to the stone foundation and the earth on the other side. The water has retreated, withdrawn. But I'm not going to let my guard down. I build a desk.

---

5 T.S. Eliot, "The Love Song of J. Alfred Prufrock."

6 Could also be Dothraki or High Elvish or Klingon. Pick your favourite.

I bring a bed down. The general who is skilled in defence hides in the most secret recesses of the earth.[7]

I have a paralegal at the firm research the permits that might be required to build a bunker below this. But that doesn't seem right. The house itself should be the bunker, should be unassailable.

How long could I last here if when ... things fall apart? Power, water ... I start preparing.

(Shift.)

(**PROJECTION**: Geography is a verb; space is an event.)

POSTDOC
Welcome to the Centre for Avant-Garde Geography.

MARK
Hi. We've met before, haven't we?

POSTDOC
Could be.

MARK
Some of the folk I met while ah eating talked about this place. They joked that "if things ever get too bad, I'll just check in to the Centre for Avant-Garde Geography, you know if it's a real place ..." Well, it is real, and I've checked in.

POSTDOC
There are essentially two facets to our work here. The physical? We want to help your body recover from whatever geomaladies are impeding you. And the mental? We want to help you understand your condition.

7 Sun Tzu, *The Art of War.*

MARK

Great. And how long does this typically ... because I really do want to get back to, you know, haha, my life.

POSTDOC

It very much depends on –

MARK

Couple weeks?

POSTDOC

Oh. (laughing) Let's get started, shall we?

This is Bachelard Oil? It's a tincture that should help with the off-balance feeling, the sliding feeling? And that should facilitate the ongoing work ... Just one or two drops? under the tongue.

MARK

... it's like music, like sad music. A bit like an empty street after rain.

POSTDOC

Okay. That's great.

MARK

Is it working?

POSTDOC

Probably?

MARK

So that's the physical, I guess.

(Shift.)

GEOTHERAPIST

Tell me about photograph you lost.

MARK

Sure. It's ah my family. A day at the beach. Years ago. We ah Julia had her big sun hat and movie-star sunglasses. She was young. We were.

Young. Then Isabel is buried in the sand. And we turned her into a mermaid, because she was fascinated by mermaids – I guess she's a siren, 'cause we gave her two tails, and we decorated them, her, with shells we collected and little grasses and flowers, and then Xavi planted his dump truck on her and everybody thought that was very funny – and that's ah that's ah the picture.

Sometimes I thought you could see – something about the angle of his head or the set of his shoulders – you can see how Xavi is going to ah the way he's going to be so private when he's older he was only four then but –

I text him every so often but ah even that feels like I'm intruding or something. When he doesn't reply, it feels like a deliberate silence like he's saying, I can't be bothered, or I could be just imagining but that's what it feels like. He used to be so ... affectionate, demonstrative ... when he was ... little.

Isabel is better about getting in touch. She replies to texts and we chat every once in a while but she ah you know she's a young woman she has her own life and –

It all fell apart somehow. I don't really understand because you know it's I don't think we were unhappy, but kids grow up, they grow away, and that changes your relationship and if you're not paying attention then ah –

The world is a big place and we're small it's easy to ah get lost or overwhelmed or ah –

I cry all the time now. I just cry. Anywhere. On airplanes, watching the movies? It doesn't matter what – *Miss Congeniality.*

GEOTHERAPIST

I have not seen this movie.

MARK

... I wanted to ... to hold on to ... my ... place. I wanted to have – I thought I could take hold of the world? My life? Not with screens and eyes but with my teeth and lips and stomach acids. It made sense. Doesn't it?

GEOTHERAPIST
What's that?

MARK
Not the frog so much maybe. I admit that was a little much. But I wanted to ingest what everybody else has.

GEOTHERAPIST
Which is?

MARK
Their place in the world?

GEOTHERAPIST
...

MARK
...

GEOTHERAPIST
You know there are millions of people in world who are displaced? Stateless, homeless, living in camps. They have no place in world, literally.

MARK
I guess. I mean, yes. I do. I'm aware.

GEOTHERAPIST
I don't mean it as criticism.

MARK
It made sense at the time.

GEOTHERAPIST
Why not write poem? If you're feeling sad.

MARK

I'm not a poet. I'm just a ... I don't know what. And I don't feel sad. I feel ... lost ... completely lost.

GEOTHERAPIST

Nostalgia.

MARK

Nostalgia?

GEOTHERAPIST

This is Greek word. From pain of returning.

MARK

Homesickness.

GEOTHERAPIST

It was originally Swiss disease. Fatal. Now everybody has it.

When I went back to Montenegro, every stone and every brick spoke to me.

MARK

Where on earth would the stones and bricks speak to me?

Look, doctor, I really need to –

(MARK's phone buzzes.)

Oh, that's my phone. Sorry.

GEOTHERAPIST

We don't encourage use of screen techn –

MARK

It's my daughter! I'm going to take this. Do you mind –

(A FaceTime call.)

MARK

HEY! It's so nice to see you.

ISABEL

Yeah, you too.

MARK

What's going on?

ISABEL

Where are you?

MARK

Me? ... I'm in my hotel.

ISABEL

Yeah. But where?

MARK

Oh. It's hard to tell sometimes. Hotel rooms ... you know they all blur together. It's easy to forget.

ISABEL

Sure. But ... where are you?

MARK

Constantinople?

ISABEL

Cool. Where is that? Greece? No, is that even a place anymore?

MARK

Yeah, no. I'm in Beirut.

ISABEL

Oh, you're back in Beirut.

MARK

No, I'm actually at the Centre for Avant-Garde Geography. Doing a thing here. Yeah. So ... what's up, darling? How are things? What's going on?

ISABEL

Avant-garde geography. That's cool.

MARK

Where are you?

ISABEL

Oh, I'm ...

MARK

That's not our – that's not your room.

ISABEL

No, I'm not at home. I'm –
I was thinking about how you taught me to swim.

MARK

Oh yeah?

ISABEL

Do you remember?

MARK

Teaching you to swim?
Sure. We were on holiday. We went to the ocean.

ISABEL

And I must have been about five? Maybe?

MARK

You were. Five.

ISABEL

And it was so huge and I was scared and we walked out, and I swallowed some water and I was so shocked you know – SALT! – and then you stuck your face in and swallowed some water too and you spat it all out and made a face and you kept doing it and doing this fake scream and making me laugh and then you carried me around, bobbing me in the water, for hours, and you said the salt that it would hold me up, and eventually you let me go, and I floated. By the end of the week, I swam out to the sand bar with you. Do you remember?

MARK
And you found a sand dollar.

ISABEL
Yeah. I remembered that. I didn't know –

MARK
Your audio is glitchy.

ISABEL
I remembered the sand dollar. And you said it was a coin that a mermaid had dropped. And that means there must be mermaids around.

MARK
Did I?

ISABEL
Yeah.
So ... are you and Mom – did you split up?

MARK
Oh. Well. Julia, she – it's a temporary ah situation so ...

ISABEL
... Dad?
You froze for a sec.

MARK
So, I'm just in rehab, kind of, just getting myself together and making some changes / so that ... Don't worry.

ISABEL

Dad? I can't – you're frozen and the sound's all funny. Did you say rehab?

MARK

Internet connection isn't great here. Can you hear me now? I'm fine. I'll be home soon, that's all.

ISABEL

I'm quitting school, Dad. I uh stopped going to practices ages ago and I'm going to go with Makambe, we're going to work for a climate- / change NGO, and I told Mom and I was thinking you were going to be home 'cause I wanted to be able to tell you in person –

MARK

Sorry honey – I didn't catch any of that. Can you hear me? I'm not getting your audio, just a really pixelated image ... Isabel?

ISABEL

Please don't try to talk me out of it, okay?

MARK

What was that?
Honey, I don't know if you can hear me ...

It's lovely to see you – even pixelated.

(Shift.)

GEOTHERAPIST

Test results have come in.

MARK

Those drops are working. I don't feel dizzy anymore.

GEOTHERAPIST

This is positive but is only symptom.

MARK

What is?

GEOTHERAPIST

You have been crashing around globe, ignoring limits of body, trying to keep up with speed of business, speed of information. But you are not money, you are not data. You are fleshy being. Biologically, we are meant to travel quite slowly, but world we live in is accelerated, and acceleration itself is accelerating. And this has consequences on organism.

MARK

Okay. So I what? I slow down? Just go slow.

GEOTHERAPIST

If only it were so simple.

MARK

What do you mean?

GEOTHERAPIST

Some people initiate movement, others do not. Some are more on receiving end of movement than others; some feel movement but go nowhere, almost in prison by movement.[8]

MARK

I'm not a stupid person but ...

GEOTHERAPIST

Labourer in Mexico, is moved by global economy, picked up by invisible hand and moved across continent, thousands of kilometres to pick your tomatoes. But tomato pickers do not decide how or when they are moved or under what conditions. What about you? Are you mover or moved?

MARK

I'm not a tomato picker. I'm a mover.

---

8 Doreen Massey, *Global Sense of Place*. Women's mobility is circumscribed by men; people in Brazilian favelas are connected to global football and club culture in London, yet have never been to Rio.

GEOTHERAPIST

Hmm. I think people you work for are movers. They put you in motion, send you across planet to buy and sell and these people enjoy benefits of this movement – movement of people of money of products of data. People like you and me, we are scramble in this movement, trying to keep up, trying to get foothold.

MARK

So... what do I do?

GEOTHERAPIST

This is, as Hamlet says, big question.

MARK

Yeah, it is. It's the Big Freaking Question. I need to get better. I need to get over this ah problem and – My marriage fell apart, right? I'm ALONE. I need to ... fix things. I need to fix things.

(Shift.)

(**JULIA** gets home from work.)

JULIA

Hellooo. Xavi? I'm hoome. Isa – No.

Just me. How did I get here? Is this my beautiful life? Don't wallow. Let's patrol the perimeter.

(A curious, dull, metallic banging from offstage.)

Rosa?

(Shift.)

EMEKA

Dear Mzungu,

I hope this email finds you well. Well, I hope it finds you as I am not sure exactly where you are. Of course email knows no geographic limits but all the same ... Where are you? How are you, friend? It has been many months since I last heard from you. I know that you and your wife have separated. I am sorry to learn of this. I know because I was briefly in touch with her when you fell ill around the time of the frog, and we have since spoken once or twice.

I don't know how you are dealing with this change – perhaps it is not as tragic as I thought at first, or perhaps this is a very difficult moment for you. I regret imposing on you in this way at this time, but you told me once that I should not hesitate to ask if you could ever be of assistance. Well, my friend, I am asking ...

Having recently paid the fees for my children's schools, I found myself staring once again into the terrible void that is my bank account, which would not have been the first time and God will provide, etc., etc., except of course there is no God since Nietzsche, none save perhaps the old African deities, and though they are old, poor, and infirm, they can still cause a great deal of trouble ...

My friend, I'll come to the point. A storm destroyed my home. I exaggerate. A storm tore the roof off the bar, which, you know, is also my home. I have repaired it as best I can, but it is a very temporary fix. The roof can be properly repaired for about eighty thousand Kenyan shillings or five hundred Euros. I am, as I mentioned earlier, insolvent. My friend, I am embarrassed to ask, but if you could see your way to lending a hand, I promise to repay you with interest as soon as I can.

Wishing you the very best,

"Archie"

MARK

Oh, Jesus. What a ...

(writing an email) Archie. I'm sorry to hear – *Do I send him five hundred Euros, that seems a little, I mean wouldn't that seem insulting if I just buy it for him?* Archie, I'm *so* sorry to hear of your predicament. Here's ... two hundred dollars towards the new roof. Forgive the brevity. I owe you a long email. Things are ... yes, complicated. Best. Mzungu.

(**MARK** pulls out his phone, thinks for a second. Audience sees a projection of his texts.)

Hey Buddy

(**MARK** deletes that.)

Hey Xav. How's things? Just thinking of you. Did you move out? LOL.

(He thinks for a second, then deletes it all.)

(Shift.)

MARK

There were tomatoes in my salad and I couldn't eat them. I looked at them, the tomatoes, and I ... imagined ... the workers who picked them. I could hear their jokes, their conversations about family and lovers back home, their prayers, their accounting, working out if they can buy a new pair of boots or a jacket or a beer, if they can send more money back home ...

Everything is more complicated now. Everything has history, velocity. Everything has tentacles.

Am I getting better? Or worse?

GEOTHERAPIST

That's very interesting.

We say there are two facets to our work here: physical and –

MARK

Yeah, the psychological.

GEOTHERAPIST

... there is maybe third aspect but ... my colleagues do not think –

Do you know this song? I left my heart in San Francisco ...

MARK

Do you mean I left something behind metaphorically?

GEOTHERAPIST

Not metaphor. Literally. I think you have left behind your soul.

MARK

... My soul?

GEOTHERAPIST

Hmmm.

MARK

I don't know ... if I believe in souls.

GEOTHERAPIST

What do you believe?

MARK

I used to believe in souls. When I was ten.

GEOTHERAPIST

Some people believe soul can become detached from body. That it must be restrained or contained. Must be weighed down with stones or held with hooks ...

MARK

You're saying, you're actually saying my soul got left behind? I should have waited for it. Like special baggage at the airport?

GEOTHERAPIST

The soul is slow moving. Like honey. But we rush across planet at incredible speeds, and this constant motion tears at fabric that attaches soul.[9] It is difficult to say when or where you might have lost it. Perhaps you traded soul without knowing.

---

9 "The speed at which we move is crucial ... the human sensory apparatus is designed to perceive and process sensory impressions while moving at about five km/h." Jan Gehl, Lotte Johansen Kaefer, and Solvejg Reigstad, "Close encounters with buildings," *Urban Design International* 11 (2006): 29–47.

MARK

I thought you people were doctors, scientists.

GEOTHERAPIST

We are social scientists.

MARK

...

GEOTHERAPIST

Many people live without soul. But if you are very careful, very lucky and quiet, soul might come back to you. There are shaman who deal with this kind of thing but we don't have. We applied for grant, but so many shaman are in private sector now.

(Shift.)

JULIA

I was in the back, checking the security cameras around/the perimeter and –

MARK

The security cameras?

JULIA

Yeah. I installed some cameras.

MARK

Oh. Okay.

JULIA

I like to have a sense of what is going on out there. I'm thinking a drone would be useful to be able to see the whole at once, or even a small helicopter.

MARK

Sure.

JULIA

So, I was out there and Rosa was –

MARK

Why?

JULIA

Why?

MARK

Why did you put cameras in?

JULIA

For security.

MARK

Right. But.

JULIA

I've made a lot of changes. To the house. I told you I floodproofed the basement, I also regraded everything, changed the entrance, built a wall, a new gate and so on, but I realized the real danger ultimately will be people. Trying to get in.

MARK

...?

JULIA

So. I'm in the backyard and Rosa was in her garden. The birds were stealing her beans, and she was out there sometimes eight hours a day, smacking a garbage-can lid to scare them off? Anyway, she fell. I saw her from the second floor of the shed lying there in the beans, so I ran over and tried to help her up, and she's so heavy. Her legs, they're all swollen, I don't know why she won't get some home care, it's not like she can't afford it. Anyway, we ended up having dinner.

MARK

Oh yeah.

JULIA

She had a giant pasta dish she'd made earlier and we sat outside and she banged the garbage-can lids and –

MARK

What did you talk about?

JULIA

Well, I don't know exactly. But we understood each other. I mean, the garden, her legs, the house. I started going over regularly. I always said we should have her over for dinner.

MARK

I know.

JULIA

You never wanted to.

She's lonely. She's all alone in her immaculate house and she just wanted company. One day she starts telling me about her kids. "Sofia, she no come. Long time. Three years no visit, no call ..." And her brother apparently is too old to drive anymore, so he can't visit. She says, "I clean clean clean why?"

MARK

That's kinda sad.

JULIA

I rubbed her feet, gave her a foot rub.

MARK

You did? That's so ... intimate.

JULIA

It was, kind of. It was special. She was so obviously in pain. Her legs, her feet, they're all swollen. They were like stones. And her toenails. ... nasty. So, I got a basin of warm water and washed her feet and clipped her nails.

MARK

Jesus.

JULIA

Yeah, kind of like Jesus. Except for the nail polish.

MARK

You did her toes?

JULIA

She loved it, and then we sat on her couch and watched Italian TV. Variety shows. That stuff is weird. Anyway, she left me her house.

MARK

Wow. What? What do you mean?

JULIA

She left me her house.

MARK

Her house?

JULIA

Yes. In her will. When she died.

MARK

Rosa died?

JULIA

Yes. Almost two months ago now.

MARK

She died and she left you – you mean, she bequeathed you her house. Like legally?

JULIA

Yes. In her will.

MARK

That's insane.

JULIA

It was quite a surprise. Her family is contesting. But the lawyers looked at it and I went through the paperwork. It's mine.

MARK

You got her house? You took her house.

JULIA

I didn't take her – She left it to me.

MARK

Because you painted her toenails.

JULIA

Because I was her friend. Because I took care of her.

MARK

... How did she die?

JULIA

Her heart.

MARK

She left you her house?

JULIA

We have two houses now. Side by side. It's perfect. We can create a much more secure perimeter with these two properties. Also, I had an intern do some research at the archives, and I'm certain there's a creek that runs under her property. It's a perfect source of water. And / the terrain –

MARK

Rosa died. She left you her house. And you want to secure the perimeter ...?

JULIA

Do you know what the second and third fundamentals of the *Art of War* are?

MARK

Who are you?

JULIA

The second fundamental is THE WEATHER and the third is the terrain.

MARK

We have two houses. You said, "We have two houses."

JULIA

Look, there's a lot you need to catch up with. I've been really thinking about preparing for the coming ... troubles. Sun Tzu says, "Invincibility lies in defence."

MARK

No. Why are you here? I thought we split up. I don't – I mean – I'm so happy you came to visit. But ...

JULIA

... I want us to get back together.

MARK

... You do?

JULIA

Yes. I want you to come back as soon as you're finished the treatment here. I don't want to be alone. I don't want to be old and alone. I want to get old with you. I was wrong.

I mean things won't be exactly as they were. Things have changed. And we have this second house. For you. You could live there and ...

(MARK says nothing.)

I want us to work things out.

You don't ...?

(MARK shakes his head.)

You don't want to?

(MARK nods and shakes his head vigorously, signalling yes and no.)

Say something would you?

MARK
I can't speak. I'm going to cry.

JULIA
Why?

MARK
Because that's what I want. That's what I want. I want that.

(Shift.)

POSTDOC
That was so nice your wife could visit last week?

MARK
You have no idea how nice.

POSTDOC
So, this will be the last time I bring your Bachelard Oil, 'cause my postdoc ends today? And I'll be leaving?

MARK
Oh, that's too bad. Or maybe that's a good thing?

POSTDOC
No, I'd like to stay on, but my funding ran out? So, who knows what's next. I've applied for a couple of other positions? ... have to wait and see. There's always Starbucks.

MARK
Oh, I'm sure you'll find something soon.

POSTDOC
I hope so. And you're going home soon?

MARK
Very soon.

POSTDOC
Well, good luck.

MARK
Thanks. You too. Good luck.

POSTDOC
Thanks? I think we could all use some.

(Shift.)

(A Zoom call.)

EMEKA
It comes around only once in a hundred years.

MARK
Oh.

EMEKA
There are many stories about it, probably none of them true. Some say it was first organized by apostates at the end of the last millennium ... a festival in anticipation of the coming of the Messiah. Almost certainly, it is simply a cabal of occultist foodies ... in any case ... the Festum Consummacionem Seculi, my friend. The Feast at the End of the World. You want in, Mzungu?

MARK
Ah ... what is it, exactly?

EMEKA
A meal like no other.

MARK
Archie, I don't think I should ...

EMEKA

My friend ...

MARK

No, Archie, I'm trying to clean up, you know. Trying to get better, and I've only got two days left here and I don't want to –

EMEKA

This is a one-time opportunity. Once in a lifetime.

MARK

The thing is ... I'm getting back together with Julia and –

EMEKA

This is wonderful news. I am so happy for you. I was worried. A man alone at your age is a terrible thing. You have no ballast. You are like a little boat tossed on the waves of life. You should go back to your wife. Your family.

MARK

Yeah. I'm going to. That's what I – that's the plan. Julia and I, we've been talking a lot, and we've really worked things out.

EMEKA

Wonderful.

MARK

And that's why I'm in treatment here and things are – I'm making changes.

EMEKA

Excellent. This is such good news.

MARK

Yes. Thank you. I'm very glad.

EMEKA

So, it is appropriate to celebrate. A final meal, then? A grand finale. Now that you are so much better and that your life is back on course. Say goodbye to all that in grand style and then back to your life.

(Shift.)

MARK

I fly to Tunis. There's a young guy waiting for me, and he's going to drive down the coast where I'll catch a boat that will take me to the island of Lampedusa. The guy says nothing for the entire drive, hours. Maybe he doesn't speak English. When we get to the port, he gives me a dirty cloth bag with something heavy in it. A gun.

Archie. He says.

What?

The gun.

He takes it. He pulls the magazine out of the handle, shows it to me. Bullets. He slides the top part of it back then pops the magazine back in it. Pulls the top part again and it clicks back into place. He's showing me how to load it. He gives it back to me and says again, Archie.

He indicates that I should stay here.

He gets back in his car, a red Hyundai, with no licence plate on the back I notice, and drives away.

I am alone. With a gun in one hand and my overnight bag in the other. I put the gun back in its bag and put that bag in my bag. Under my pyjamas.

JILANI

Welcome in Tunisia.

MARK

Thank you.

JILANI

I am captain of boat for you.

(JILANI reaches for MARK's bag, but MARK hangs on to it.)

MARK

It's okay.

JILANI

Come. Long trip. Ten hours. You like ocean?

(JILANI laughs.)

MARK

It's a fishing boat, a bit rusted and sad. I don't think there's anyone else on it. Just his son, I guess? The crew. The son avoids me. Do they know I have a gun? Do they have guns?

JILANI

Better than fishing.

MARK

This is better than fishing?

JILANI

No more fishes. Too little fishes now.

MARK

Oh.

JILANI

Before one day fishing: three hundred dinar; now, two, three days: one hundred fifty dinar. No good.

(JILANI spits over the rail.)

MARK

No, that's not good. That's like a 75 percent loss.

JILANI

But boat is good for many things, hamdullah.

MARK

Oh, sure, yeah.

JILANI

Smuggler is good money.

MARK

Smuggling? I guess it is.

JILANI

Very good. One ride on boat maybe five thousand dinar.

MARK

Oh. That is good.

He's a smuggler? Is that what he's saying? He definitely has a gun.

What does he smuggle?

Oh. I get it. Me. I'm … the smugglee.

(JILANI laughs at MARK and slaps him on the back.)

I lie on my cot and look at my gun. It's a Zlock. "The Polish Glock," it says on the barrel. Gen4, 9×19. A gun is a door. To another world. The world of guns. One day the world has no guns in it, and the next, it's full of guns. So many people, I realize, have guns. And they've been here all along. Alongside those of us who don't or didn't have guns. The unarmed. The sleepwalkers.

(Shift to JULIA shopping.)

JULIA

I want to be prepared for any eventuality.

SALES ASSOCIATE

Sounds about right.

JULIA

Preparation is key.

SALES ASSOCIATE

Gotta move with the times.

JULIA

Exactly.

SALES ASSOCIATE

Okay, there are a few options. We want to find the one that is right for you. Do you want something that will fit in a purse, for example?

JULIA

I don't think so. I don't want one of those girly ones.

SALES ASSOCIATE

Something a little more substantial then. Let's start with these two: the Hellcat and the Shield.

They're both 9 mm. The Hellcat is a little bigger, but very comfortable in the hand, and she packs an impressive fourteen rounds. The Shield is a little smaller, very easy to use, the slide is just buttery – try that.

(JULIA holds the pistol and racks the slide.)

JULIA

Oh, that is quite buttery, yes.

(Shift.)

MARK

When we dock, there seems to be a commotion at the harbour. There's a crowd shouting, pointing, people running. Sirena! Sirena! Someone keeps shouting. They're calling the police or there's some sort of alarm or –

There's a driver waiting for me. Archie really is a logistical genius. If he was in North America, he'd be crushing it.

I ask the driver if he knows what the commotion dockside was about. He has no idea. We pass a road that is blocked off with an imposing gate and four soldiers standing guard.

What is that?

Refugee Welcome Centre, my driver tells me.

I'm staying at the Hotel Lighea, which my driver says is named after a character from a novella from the area. The Professor and the Siren. *Which is interesting but I'm not interested. I just want the feast.*

When it's completely dark, we set off. We drive with the lights off, which seems odd but I'm more concerned about where to put Zlockie. In movies, guys tuck guns into their waistbands, but that seems very uncomfortable to me, so right now Zlockie is in my jacket pocket, but that makes a kind of awkward bulge. I should get a holster maybe, a shoulder holster.

We drive up to another one of those imposing gates like the one we passed earlier. The driver speaks to the guard and the guard shines his flashlight on me and indicates I should get out of the car. He scans my passport with his phone. There are lots of people gathered here already. Hundreds maybe.

They make us surrender our phones, but we can keep our guns.

We walk in long, snaking lines, following people carrying torches, flaming torches, which strikes me as a little silly. The ground is uneven, people keep stumbling. There are some women in heels and even some folks in wheelchairs, but a couple of guards or assistants finally help them out.

We walk into the side of a hill. Looks like a mouth. It's a giant hall, like an airplane hangar, but underground.

We're almost all men at this meal. And I'd say there's somebody here from almost every corner of the earth. Nobody says much. People are focused, maybe nervous, I know I am. This is it. The Feast. There's shouting suddenly, an altercation, at one end of the hall. One of the servers, or guards, punches a diner in the throat, hard, and the guy crumples, just goes down, and they drag him out. He snuck a phone in somehow is what people are saying, was trying to take pictures.

The plates are bone-white. No. The plates are bone. That's bone. The plate is made of bone.

The first course is an assortment of songbirds, mostly endangered, drowned in Armagnac, fried in their own fat.

Vegetarians eat rare grains stolen from peasants in the Peruvian highlands and salads composed from delicate algaes and mosses that take a hundred years to grow. Some people are eating coelacanth. Others eat auroch and passenger pigeon and dodo, creatures that have been back-bred, or genetically derived, by insatiable scientists using the latest gene-splicing technology.

People are throwing up. There seem to be brass buckets specifically for this. The vomit is vibrant, colourful, but that may be just a trick of the light. Then they keep eating.

I lose track of the courses. New plate. On a bed of seaweed is a large, wedge-shaped, iridescent something. The server says it's marvirino but I don't know what that is. The skin is tough, scaly, and there's a dense meat beneath that, massive, thick. Some sort of fish? There are little hairs in the skin too. Fine, downy hairs. I can't cut the skin so I peel it away with my knife to get at the meat beneath. It's firm like tuna. I chew carefully trying to parse the flavours: at first, there's a kind of oily, buttery fatness, then sharp sea salt but eventually a sweetness comes through, a wondrous musical sweetness. It tastes something like pork. And with each contraction of my jaws, the flavours flood me with sound, wavering voices, shifting in and out of harmony. A singing pig fish maybe. Don't some anthropophagi call human meat "long pig"? That's kind of funny. There is something oddly human about the hairs that appear between the scales, like the soft hair on Julia's arms.

Siren. I'm eating siren.

I have an erection. I retch into the bucket.

(MARK passes out.)

(Shift.)

JULIA

I admit I'm surprised that I bought a gun. I don't quite recognize myself. What does this mean, this gun? I felt quite strongly that it was necessary but ...

(JULIA looks down the barrel of the gun.)

That's where the bullet comes out. It's like a tunnel, or an eye that doesn't blink. Down that tunnel, in that eye, I see the whole property, at once, from every angle and perspective. Like the view from a thousand drones. I don't see Xavi or Isabel or my mother or Mark who should be here by now, but I do see the sky above, and the earth below, the soil, the roots and fungal networks. I see my property on the face of the turning earth and the mountains, the scorched and the safe, the islands and oceans. I see the wind, and lightning, and the moon and stars. I see through the gun's eye what seems like the whole world in all its variety, with all the forms of life and time and nature and action and hopes, and my own city and myself. There am I.

All is as it should be.

So that's why I bought the gun.

(Shift.)

(A phone call.)

MARK

Archie. Archie. I'm ... not good. I'm on a beach. I don't know how I ended up here? I've – I don't know. I don't feel well at all.

EMEKA

Hmmm.

MARK

I feel just awful. My head is killing me. I can't stand up.

EMEKA

You overindulged.

MARK
Is someone coming to pick me up?

EMEKA
I don't know.

MARK
Can you send someone?

EMEKA
...

MARK
Archie?

EMEKA
... I'm about to board a plane.

MARK
Sorry?

EMEKA
You'll have to manage on your own.

MARK
I can't walk. I can't even focus. I don't think I have my passport.

EMEKA
No, but you have your phone.

MARK
Yeah but I need my –

EMEKA
And you have your gun.

MARK
Yeah, why did you get why do I need –

EMEKA

You also have two hundred fourteen dollars in the breast pocket of your jacket.

MARK

Two hundred –

EMEKA

And fourteen. I calculated a generous 20 percent interest per annum –

MARK

Two hundred? What am I supposed to do with that?

EMEKA

Invest it? Build yourself a humble shelter?

MARK

Where's my passport? Where's my wallet? I don't have any ID, my credit cards.

EMEKA

No. But you have much more than I had when I made my way to Kenya.

MARK

Archie, what is going on?

EMEKA

There is a welcome centre for migrants on the island. Make your way there. Perhaps they can help.

MARK

Get me out of here. Send someone.

EMEKA

My flight is boarding.

MARK

Where are you going? You can't leave me here.

EMEKA

But I can. It's not personal, Mzungu.

MARK

Archie! What –

EMEKA

Save your strength and your battery. You're going to need them.

MARK

Arch – Listen, listen. Please. You can't just leave me here. I – I can help you. I can – I've been thinking. I can get you a job maybe.

EMEKA

I don't want a job, Mzungu. I want a life. And I found one that might suit me.

(EMEKA puts his phone away.)

MARK

Archie! Archie!

EMEKA

It's not personal, O. It's just business.

I admit, at first, I dey very angry. I been vex well well. Mzungu could have easily built me a new roof one hundred times over! Abeg! How much did he pay to poison himself with the frog? And yes, I vex at myself well well. How long it took me to write that email. To work up my courage. To ASK for help and then to be slapped in the face with two hundred dollars. I was compelled to face with sober senses the real conditions of my life and my relations with Mzungu and with others.

In business school, we read case studies of successful entrepreneurs. So we could learn the subtleties of their thinking, their strategies. But there really wasn't much strategy, just a lot of luck.

One fellow, from the US, had a food-packing facility, and a small part of their business was preparing meals for the military. A little contract, a few thousand dollars. Then one day the US attacks Iraq and the government suddenly wants them to produce millions of these meals. Iraq gets blown to pieces and he makes a fortune. He just happened to be there. Right place, right time. Luck.

And so with Mzungu. He was the opportunity I'd been waiting for. And I took it. It's just business. Or if you are of a more philosophical bent, think of me as the long slow arc of history. Or the face of the future.

(ISABEL appears.)

ISABEL

Dear Mom and Dad,

I hope this finds you.

A lot has happened. We almost died. Makambe and me.

We ran into a storm when there weren't supposed to be any, but this is a planet of storms now. They come and go as they please. The boat was being thrown up and down. Everything was shaking and the waves were tall as houses. I can't tell you what it's like to look up and see water where you should see sky. It's an ancient, dark feeling from when everything was alive with gods. Makambe says there's a thing in the Bible that those who go to the sea in ships know the works and power of God or something and it's true. Not the Bible God but the sea is alive and it is a god.

I thought this can't be happening to me. It wasn't fair because I've barely lived, and I was trying to do something good, you know, I was one of the good guys. White saviour complex, right? I thought, I can't drown, that would be too stupid. I didn't know where Makambe was, but I prayed she got into one of the lifeboats, and I just tried to follow the waves. Not fight. Survive.

I thought I could see lights. Tiny tiny lights. And I tried to swim to them for hours, but I couldn't make any progress, and I started swallowing water and I knew I was getting exhausted. I realized the sea didn't care about me; I understood how puny I really am in the scheme of things, and it didn't matter, in a sort of profound way, whether I lived or died, and it was just an illusion this feeling of being important. It wasn't exactly peaceful, but I understood something kind of total ... I understood how things *really* are. I can't explain it, and ever since I've been trying to feel it again to understand.

(Shift. JULIA comes home. Puts her bag on the table. Stops. Something is off.)

JULIA
Xavi?

(JULIA listens.)

Xavi, are you home?

(JULIA slowly pulls her gun from her bag.)

(EMEKA appears.)

EMEKA
Hello. I'm sorry to startle you.

JULIA
How did you get in here?

EMEKA
Your son let me in.

JULIA
Xavi? (calling out) Xavi?

EMEKA
He was on his way out. He's not home.

JULIA
You're ... Chukwuemeka, aren't you? What are you ...? Nice to meet you in person.

EMEKA
A pleasure to meet you as well.

JULIA

You look different in person – not on FaceTime, I mean. Oh, I'm sorry, let me put (gesturing to her gun) this away.

(Shift.)

ISABEL

I woke up in a hut. In a village. A fishing village on the island of Ixturria. It's not down on any map. True places never are. They found me and Makambe and took care of us and we live here now.

The people here are fishers. They go out every day in their green-and-blue boats. Makambe and I go too. We're learning. We catch a lot of fish I don't recognize and also sea cucumber and sometimes a shark, which is worth quite a lot of money. There are so many beautiful children, and they go to school, and everyone helps clean the catch. The fishers all have bad backs from lifting those incredibly heavy nets so it's not paradise but it's green even if there's a lot of plastic getting caught in the nets and the water is rising, 'cause you can see the little shelters where they clean the fish some of them are in the water now, and they had to build new ones farther up the beach.

We live in a little hut. Everybody helped us put it together. It's raised off the ground a bit and has a thatched roof. A big storm could maybe tear the roof off or sweep the whole thing away. It's precarious. Not just the hut, I mean, everything here. I don't think you'd approve. It's not particularly ambitious. The people here don't think about more or progress or ... I think that's right. I think we need to get over more and progress if we want to survive.

I'm not criticizing you, it's just a decision or an understanding. I'm trying to live smaller, trying to live closer to things, to plants and fish and water and others. Makambe says the word "precarious" comes from the word "prayer," like if you're precarious you're living on a prayer, and I think that's honest, an honest way to live now. That's where we are now.

I just went for a swim. I found a sand dollar. The waves are really gentle right now. The water is actually glowing, from plankton and stuff, and farther out there are jellyfish that glow and then all the fish and dolphins and whales. The breeze is stirring the palm trees so they all whisper together, and way above them are the stars, they're so bright here, and so many. And somewhere there must be a mermaid looking for the coin she dropped. It's so clear to me that the earth is actually conscious and so much bigger and wiser than us. And of course I don't want anybody to die or suffer, but I can see that the planet is going to be okay without us. I'd like to see it but.

(ISABEL on the beach; EMEKA and JULIA drink wine; MARK crawls slowly across the sand.)

ACKNOWLEDGMENTS

Thanks to:

The Canadian Association for Theatre Research for inviting me to give the keynote that became this play.

Andy McKim and Theatre Passe Muraille.

Matt McGeachy and Factory Theatre.

Brendan Healey and Canstage.

Mike Payette and Tarragon Theatre.

Dr. Ben Akoh for his generous assistance with Nigerian cultural specifics (any errors remain my responsibility).

And my friends and colleagues whose support made all the difference: Daniel Brooks, Karen Hines, Matthew MacKenzie, and, most of all, Sina X Gilani.

Special thanks are due Thomas Morgan Jones for his generous, gentle, and expert leadership throughout the development and production process.

GUILLERMO VERDECCHIA is a writer of drama and fiction as well as a director, dramaturge, translator, and actor. He is the recipient of a Governor General's Award for Drama for his play *Fronteras Americanas* and a four-time winner of the Chalmers Canadian Play Award. His work includes the critically acclaimed *Feast*, *The Art of Building a Bunker* (with Adam Lazarus), the Governor General–shortlisted *Noam Chomsky Lectures* (with Daniel Brooks), the Seattle Times' Footlight Award–winning *Adventures of Ali & Ali* (with Marcus Youssef and Camyar Chai), *A Line in the Sand* (with Marcus Youssef), *bloom*, and *Another Country*. His work has been recorded, anthologized, translated into Spanish and Italian, and produced in Europe and the US, and is studied in Latin America, Australia, Europe, and North America.